www.bonnieleebooks.com

Printed in China

ISBN:0-9883015-6-6

THE DOWN UNDER SALAD BOWL

Karri Koala comes from Australia.

The Australian Flag looks like the night sky.

WEST
AUSTRA

PERTH

Australia is an island; it is the biggest island in the world!
Australia also has the largest desert in the world called The Outback.

DARWIN

NORTHERN
TERRITORY

QUEENSLAND

SOUTH
AUSTRALIA

BRISBANE

NEW SOUTH
WALES

ADELAIDE

SYDNEY

CANBERRA

VICTORIA

MELBOURNE

A

TASMANIA

N

W   E

S

I'm a koala,
not a koala bear.
I look like a teddy bear
but I'm a marsupial.

Marsupials carry their babies in a pouch on the mother's belly.

The name "marsupial" comes from the Latin word "marsupium" which means "pouch".

Kimba the Tasmanian Devil

Bitsy the Sugar Glider

Casper the Cuscus

Nurla the Numbat

See my big nose?
I can smell the best tasting
eucalyptus leaves with this nose.
I love eucalyptus leaves.

Karri don't be so picky,
have a taste of something new!

Okay I tried!
Now it's time to eat what I love!
Eucalyptus leaves!
YUM!

Coloring Time!

KOALA
Scientific Name: *Phascolarctos cinerus*

NORTHERN HAIRY-NOSED WOMBAT

Scientific Name: *Lasiorhinus kretii*

PLATYPUS
Scientific Name: *Orinthorhynchus anatinus*

Bonnie Lee Books

bonnieleebooks.com